The Museum

Contents

CHILLERS

The Museum

Brandon Robshaw

Published in association with
The Basic Skills Agency

Hodder & Stoughton

A MEMBER OF THE HODDER

Acknowledgements
Cover: Dave Smith
Illustrations: Jim Eldridge

Orders; please contact Bookpoint Ltd, 39 Milton Park, Abingdon, Oxon OX14
4TD. Telephone: (44) 01235 400414, Fax: (44) 01235 400454. Lines are open
from 9.00–6.00, Monday to Saturday, with a 24 hour message answering service.
Email address: orders@bookpoint.co.uk

British Library Cataloguing in Publication Data
A catalogue record for this title is available from the British Library

ISBN 0 340 77259 X

First published 2000
Impression number 10 9 8 7 6 5 4 3 2 1
Year   2005 2004 2003 2002 2001 2000

Typeset by GreenGate Publishing Services, Tonbridge, Kent.
Printed in Great Britain for Hodder & Stoughton Educational, a division of
Hodder Headline Plc, 338 Euston Road, London NW1 3BH, by Atheneum
Press, Gateshead, Tyne & Wear

1

The Burial

The moon was full.
In the distance,
wolves were howling.

Two men carried the dead man
down to the marsh.
The whole tribe followed.
They wore animal skins
and their faces were painted.
They sang slow, sad songs
as they walked.

The dead man had been their King.
His son walked in front, his head low.
Next to him walked the medicine man
of the tribe.

At the edge of the marsh,
they dug a grave.
They put the dead man in it.
Around him, they placed food,
stone weapons and tools
and water in a stone jar.
He would need these things in the next life.

The medicine man
sang magic words
over the grave.
The dead man's son wept.

Then they walked back
to the forest.
'Where is my father now?' asked the son.

'He is wandering in the country of the dead,'
said the medicine man.
'But one day, he will come back.
A great and royal spirit like your father's
is sure to come back.
He will take another body
to house his spirit.'

'When?' asked the son.
He sounded scared.

'He will not trouble you,' said the medicine
man.
'It will not be in our time.'

They reached their home in the forest.
That night, there was feasting.

And twenty thousand years went by.

2

Stone Age Tony

Twenty thousand years, thought Dave.
It was a long time.
He looked down at the body
in the glass case.
Stone Age Tony, they called him.

Stone Age Tony lay on his side,
just as he had been found in the marsh.
The peat in the marsh
had stopped the body from rotting.

His skin was like brown leather.
You could still see tufts of blond hair
on his head.
His teeth were bared in a grin.
Only his eyes had gone,
leaving dark, empty sockets.

Around the body lay the objects
that had been found with it –
stone weapons and tools
and a stone jar.

Dave liked working in the museum.
He had only just started there –
he'd left school last summer.

He had always liked history.
He liked the Roman room
and the Victorian room
and the armour from the Middle Ages.
But he liked Stone Age Tony best of all.
To see the body of a real person
from the Stone Age –
it was amazing.

The public thought so too.
There was always a little crowd
round Stone Age Tony's case.

But the public had all gone home now.
It was six o'clock,
time to close for the night.

His boss, the museum's curator,
had already gone home.
The museum shop had closed.
No one was left but Dave.
It was his job to lock up.

'Good night, Tony!' he said to the body
in the glass case.
He always said this.
There was no answer, of course.

As he was about to lock the main door,
Dave heard a noise.
A noise of something moving.
It seemed to come from the Stone Age room.
Dave stopped.
He felt himself shiver.
What could be moving?

He listened.
But all was quiet now.
'Must have imagined it', Dave said to himself.
He locked up and went home.

3

'Who's there?'

Dave knew something was wrong
as soon as he opened up
the next morning.

As he stepped inside the museum,
he heard a noise again.
A noise of something moving.

'Who's there?' called Dave.
No answer.

The noise seemed to come from
the Stone Age room.
Dave ran in and
looked into Stone Age Tony's case.
He got the shock of his life.

Stone Age Tony had moved.
His head had turned so that
he was staring up at the ceiling.
His arms were in a new position.
The stone tools and weapons
around him had been moved, too.

A chill ran through Dave.
He stood frozen to the spot
for a moment.
Then he backed slowly out of the room.

In the doorway,
he bumped into
someone.

Dave screamed.

4

Strange Goings On

'Steady on!' said a voice.
It was Mr Jackson, his boss.
'What's the matter?'

'In … in there!' gasped Dave.
'Stone Age Tony …
he's moved!'

'What are you talking about?'
Mr Jackson marched up to the glass case
and looked in.

His face grew very serious.
'Who did this?'

'No one,' said Dave.
'No one's been in here since last night.
He must have moved himself!'

'Don't be stupid!' said Mr Jackson.
'He's been dead for twenty thousand years.
Someone must have broken in.
Didn't you see anything?
Hear anything?'

'Well, now I think of it,' said Dave slowly,
'I did hear a noise last night.
When I was locking up.'

'That's it, then,' said Mr Jackson.
'Someone hid in here last night
and messed about with him.'

'Why didn't I see them this morning?'

'They must have run out
when you weren't looking.'

'But why would anyone mess about
with Stone Age Tony?' asked Dave.
'It's – it's disgusting.'

'There are some funny people about,'
said Mr Jackson.
'Some very funny people.
You'd better keep your eyes open.
Check there's no one hanging about
when you lock up tonight.'

5

The Police Arrive

Dave checked every room
before he locked up that night.
There was nobody there.

'Good night, Tony,' he said.
It made him angry to think of
someone messing about with the body.
They should show some respect for the dead.
Well, they wouldn't be able to do it again.
The museum was empty now, he was sure.
He locked the door.
Stone Age Tony would have a peaceful night.

But Dave was wrong.

When he opened up the next morning,

he smelt a strange, heavy smell,

like damp earth.

He went into the Stone Age room.

The lid of Stone Age Tony's case was open.

There were pieces of earth on the floor.

Dave called Mr Jackson.

'Look!' he said.

'They've been here again.

And this time, it looks like

they've had him out of the case!'

'I told you to double-check last night!'

said Mr Jackson.

'I did!' said Dave.
'They must have broken in somehow.'

'We'd better call the police,' said Mr Jackson.
The police came,
but could find no signs of a break-in.

'It beats me how they're getting in,'
said the sergeant.
'Maybe someone should stay
and keep watch tonight.'

'That's a good idea,' said Mr Jackson.

'I'll do it,' said Dave.
It made his blood boil to think of someone
messing about with poor old Tony.
He'd love to catch them at it.
He'd teach them a lesson
they wouldn't forget.

6

Night Watch

The last visitor had gone.
The museum was as quiet
as an empty church.
The full moon shone in through the windows.

Dave had a torch,
but was careful to keep it pointing down.
He didn't want to scare the intruders off.
He wanted to catch them at it.
He had taken his shoes off, too,
so that his footsteps wouldn't make a noise.

The hours passed slowly.
Dave walked from room to room,
listening.
Then, at about two o'clock,
Dave heard a sound.
A sound of someone moving.

He ran into the Stone Age room.
He shone his torch at the glass case
where Stone Age Tony lay.

Dave's heart missed a beat.

The case was empty.

7

Footsteps in the Hall

For a moment, Dave didn't move.
He didn't know what to do.
His mind was a blank.

Then he heard footsteps.
They were coming from the main hall.
Dave ran in and saw a figure
in the moonlight.

It was walking slowly, painfully,
towards the main door.
It fumbled at the door handle,
trying to open it.

'Hoy!' shouted Dave.
He ran towards the figure.
It turned round.
Dave shone his torch
in the figure's face.

The face had brown, leathery skin.
There were tufts of blond hair on its head.
Its teeth were bared in a grin.
Its eye sockets were empty and dark.

It was Stone Age Tony.
With arms stretched out in front of him,
he began to walk towards Dave.

8

Trapped!

Dave backed away.
Stone Age Tony's head turned
to follow him.
Somehow, out of those dark, empty sockets,
he was able to see Dave.

Dave found that he had backed up
against the wall.
He was trapped.
Stone Age Tony got nearer and nearer.

He said something
in a low voice.
Dave didn't understand it.
In his own language, Stone Age Tony
was saying, 'At last!'

He grabbed Dave by the shoulders.
His touch felt cold and leathery.
His empty eye sockets stared at Dave.

Dave was too frightened to move
or cry out.
He felt that he was getting dizzy.
Then everything went black.

9

All Alone

Some time later, Dave awoke.
He seemed to be lying down.
He tried to get up, but couldn't move.

He looked up.
Standing over him,
he saw himself.

He saw himself smiling.

At once, Dave knew what had happened.
Somehow, Stone Age Tony
had swapped bodies with him.
He, Dave, was now a thing of leathery skin
in a glass case.
He couldn't move, he couldn't talk.

But Stone Age Tony could talk.
'Good night, Tony,' he said
and laughed.
He's taken my voice, too,
thought Dave.

Dave heard footsteps walking away.
He heard the main door open and close.
He was left alone.

The night passed.
Then it was day.
People came to the museum
and looked down at Dave
in his glass case.

Stone Age Tony didn't come back
to the museum.
'I wonder what he's doing
now that he's got my body',
thought Dave.
But there was no way of finding out.

Then the day was over.
Another night passed.

Then there was another day …